Ship Rats

A Tale of Heroism on the High Seas

Rat Tales, Part One

By Rhian Waller

Printed in the UK

First Printing, 2017

ISBN 978-0-244-30857-5

Cover image by @Tofu_Soup

Inside illustrations by Gill Thomas

Maps drawn by Rhian Waller with reference
to the Mercator map.

With thanks to the crew who helped plug the leaks in this story and keep it shipshape. To Barrie, Ato, Teddy, Alex, Róisín, Michael and my mother, who have shared (or at least put up with) my growing rat obsession.

Dedicated to Leeloo, Priss and Ripley, the rescue rats who started the obsession in the first place.

Characters

Rats

Lu: a friendly, trusting white rat. She is just over one month old when her adventure starts

Rip: Lu's calm, collected older sister

Preen: The middle sister. She frets a lot and likes to be tidy

Pew: A smelly but cunning old rat

Sleek: A messenger-rat for Black Spot

Black Spot: The Skipper of the rats. He hates and fears humans

Thug: A very large, strong rat who lives on the *Hydromyst*

Bigs

Runa: A young Swedish girl who is determined to find her Pa

The Captain: A Dutch man. He is in charge of the ship and all of the crew. He keeps his jacket buttons shiny

The Bosun: The officer in charge of anchors, sails, ropes and rigging. He is jolly

The First Mate: The second in command after the Captain. He is trustworthy and true

The Second Mate: The third in command. He likes a stiff drink

Sections

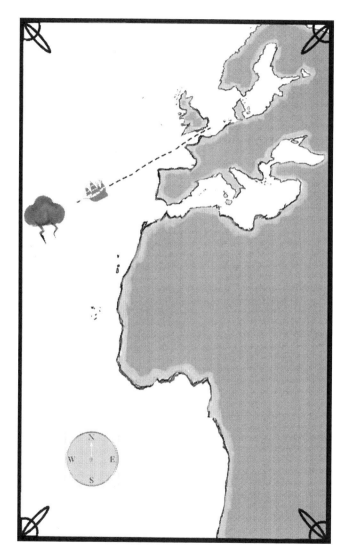

The Hydromyst sails into a storm...

Author's Note

Thank you for picking up my book, dear reader. Before we begin, I must admit I used to be afraid of rats. I thought they were dirty. They made me jump. I worried they might bite me. Then I found the writings of a certain young naturalist who spent a great deal of time observing three particular rats – and I learned a lot about them.

I pieced together the story of their travels. Of course I have taken some liberties but the core of the tale is true. Nothing that takes place in this book is beyond what an ordinary rat could do.

Rats are prone to adventure because they are brave and bright. They are also small enough to pick up in one hand. When you are that size, even crossing a room can be a challenge.

This book is the first in a series of stories about three ratty sisters. I hope you enjoy them and learn to look past what you believe of rats to see what they really are.

1: Home nest

There were eight babies to begin with. When their mother realised they were about to be born, she retreated to her safe nest in the wall of the Customs building in the Dutch port of Vernaya. The nest was a soft place to give birth as it was lined with yellow paper stolen from the clerk's desks and stuffing nibbled free from the chair in the boss' office.

The baby rats lay in the paper, all cuddled up and warm. They looked like pink jellybeans. Five of them were boys and three were girls.

Mum Rat named her girls Rip, Preen and Lu. They had to be short names because rats can only manage small, squeaky words.

Their eyes opened when they were two weeks old and then Mum Rat had a job on her paws because they started to explore. Their world broadened from warm, milky softness to something larger.

Rip, who was the biggest rat, had fur that was a rich brown. She was calm and did not enjoy playing or fighting. Preen, who was the middle rat, had grey fur that ran from her face right over her back to her tail. She was pretty and spent a lot of time washing. Lu, the smallest sister, was almost pure white except for when her fur was a bit scruffy. She was the friendliest but also rather silly.

Their brothers were lazy and happy to sleep. Their names were Stretch, Snore, Snooze, Snug and Kip.

Lu was the first to waddle out of the nest on unsteady paws and find the gap in the wall while Mum Rat was busy grooming Rip. Lu stuck her nose out.

There were all sorts of interesting smells in the Customs Office. This was where sailors and their passengers declared their cargo. Sometimes they had to present the things they carried across the sea in their ships and boats. They brought in samples of tobacco, exotic drinks, whiffy cheeses, animal skins and plants from the other side of the world. Lu could also smell ink, paper and people. She could see the dim outlines of furniture.

She wanted to explore.

Rats communicate in lots of ways. They use quiet sounds, too high-pitched for a human to hear, and they also talk through their whiskers, twitching ears and through touch. They only squeak loudly when they are scared, angry or want to get attention. So Lu jumped when she heard her name.

'Lu!' It was her mother. 'No. Stop.'

Mum Rat used her body to push Lu back to the nest.

'What's out there?' said Preen, later, when Mum Rat had gone in search of food and the little ones were too sleepy and full of milk to think about running off.

'Strange things,' said Lu.

'Good things?' said Preen.

'No,' said Rip, who listened to Mum Rat. 'Bad things. Risk. Fear. There are Bigs out there.'

To rats, humans are giants. That's why they call us 'Bigs'.

Lu wasn't so sure the world outside was bad. It was broad and busy but it was also interesting.

'Go to sleep,' said Mum Rat, so Lu curled up and tried to do as she was told. But she could not sleep; she was too busy wondering about the world.

Rittens (that is, baby rats) grow up fast and Lu got bigger. Her curiosity grew too.

Mum Rat kept all eight of her children close. She taught them the three things all rittens should know. These are rules that, all together, are known as *kree*. They are there to make sure that rats, who can live in huge colonies, know how to get along - and they are still used to this day.

The first rule is that, no matter how bitter the argument or how vicious the fight, rats will forgive each other swiftly.

The second rule is that rats look out for each other. They might squabble over food, but they also help clean each other and stay together. If a rat is caught in a cage her friends will help her get out - if they can.

The third rule is about manners. Rats should always politely sniff-sniff on meeting to learn about each other.

Of course, rats don't use human words. All of the rat conversations have been changed so you can understand them. The lesson sounded like this: *'Peep, peep, wuppa-wuppa meep woop peep!'*, which obviously doesn't make much sense to us.

Lu understood her mother, but she wanted to know about outside as well.

'You should stay here,' said Mum Rat, who worried about Lu the most. The little ritten had ruby red eyes. Sometimes she swayed her head from side to side to see better, which made it look like she was disagreeing about something, even though she was the friendliest baby Mum Rat had ever had. Her poor eyesight made it even more dangerous out in the wide world; white rats did not often last long without becoming dinner for a cat or another kind of hunter.

'But I don't want to stay!' said Lu. 'I want to be out there.'

'Stay with me,' said Mum Rat. 'You will be safe.'

'What is safe?' said Rip.

'Safe is when you don't get hurt,' said Mum Rat. 'You are safe with me, which is good. Keep away from things that are not safe, like Bigs.'

'What is a Big?' said Preen.

'Bigs are the things with two legs that move out there in the day. They are loud and tall,' said Rip, who was wiser than her sisters.

'What if we won't stay safe?' said Lu, who was not afraid of Bigs.

'Dad Rat did not stay safe,' said Mum Rat. 'That is why a Cat got him. I do not want the Cat to get you.'

'What is a Cat?' said Preen. She shivered. Only frightening or important things were spoken about in capital letters.

'A Cat is a beast with sharp teeth and claws. Cats eat us,' said Mum Rat.

But Lu saw no sign of a cat outside.

One day, when she was about a month and a half old, she could not wait any longer. Lu was ready to run. She sneaked out of the nest and scurried through the hole. Rip watched her go.

'Lu is daft,' she yawned.

Preen stood up.

'I want to see where she goes,' she said.

'Stay. It's time to wash,' said Rip.

'But I want to see.'

Rip made a chirp of annoyance. As the biggest and oldest ritten by a whole five minutes she thought it was her job to look after her sisters. She got up and followed Lu and Preen. Their brothers just lazed and rolled over into the warm space. That was what kept them safe on that fateful night and is why this book is not about them. Don't worry though; they would have their own adventures one day.

Lu, meanwhile, was finding things out.

She kept low and close to the wall. It was night and the Customs Office was empty.

Lu's eyes were not strong but her nose, ears and nerves were alert.

Everything was so huge! She hadn't known anything could be as wide as this. The walls went up forever. The desks were mountains and the floor was a vast field made of planks.

Nothing bad happened. No cats or owls grabbed Lu. There were no loud noises or flashes of light. She grew braver.

Lu climbed up a desk. She found a piece of paper. It was an important document but Lu didn't know that. She grabbed it in her teeth, fell off the desk and ran across the floor, giggling. Once there she was so excited she went in circles, still holding the paper so it covered her body. If a Big had seen it they might have thought the room was haunted.

Then Lu got bored and dropped the paper because she smelled crumbs. A worker had eaten a sandwich and left some on the floor. Lu found it and ate it fast. Preen joined her and they squabbled over the bread.

'Shh,' said Rip. 'You make too much noise.'

But Preen and Lu were having fun. They pretended to fight. Lu climbed up a cabinet to escape and knocked some books on the floor. They fell with a clatter. The rats froze.

Nothing happened for a very long time from Lu's point of view. Rats live fast. Their hearts beat ten times quicker than a human's.

Lu started to relax. Then the rats heard a key in the lock.

The door opened.

There was noise and light.

A guard came in.

Lu looked far up into a huge face. It hung like a pink moon.

The Big walked into the office. His footsteps were thunder. He lifted the lantern in his hand, dazzling the rats. He went past them. Now he was between them and the hole that led back to the nest.

'The Big will find us!' squeaked Preen.

'This way!' said Lu.

'No, go back!' said Rip, who wanted to get home.

'No time!' said Lu and just then the Big shone his light on the three scampering sisters. He made a loud noise.

Lu dashed away. She ran to the open door.

She could feel cold against her fur. She smelled salt, water and space. It was too late to stop. She hurtled out of the Customs Office and found herself running over smooth flagstones. She was outside!

Chapter 2: The Outside

Lu pressed against the wall and stopped running. The air was different. It moved more. Wood creaked and water slapped against stone. There were other Bigs moving around but they were quite far away. She panted.

Where were Preen and Rip?

Lu realised she was alone. Her tail drooped and she made herself small. She was afraid. She had never been alone before. It's easier to be brave when you have someone beside you.

She made a sad little 'meep'.

'Shush!'

Lu jumped. The wind was blowing so she hadn't heard or smelled the new rat.

He was big and brown with holes in his ears. One of his eyes was closed. He was also very, very ancient.

Lu sniffed his nose to say hello. He smelled at least three years old.

She was still scared but even a strange rat was better than being alone. He seemed trustworthy, in a musty, ripe way.

'Yarr,' he said. His teeth were yellow and stumpy.

There was a bang behind them. The Big guard had not found anything suspicious in the Customs Office. Rats were common at the harbour. He shut and locked the door.

'I want to go home,' said Lu.

'It be too late,' said the old rat. 'There ain't no way back now. Not through that door.'

Actually, there were holes and cracks in many of the buildings but Lu did not know where they were. Nor, it turned out, did the old rat. He wasn't from the harbour.

'Cheer up,' he said, trying to be kind.

Lu could not be happy. Too much had happened too fast. She was lost. But she was a bold little rat and she pulled herself together to think.

'Who are you?'

'I be Pew,' said the old rat. 'Why did ye run here?'

'A Big shone a light on me and made noise.'

Pew made a rat snigger.

'The Bigs be slow. There is no need to fear. Be fleet and smart and they can't catch ye. I live with Bigs,' he said airily. 'They don't know I be there.'

'Oh?'

'Aye. I be slow now, but still smart.' He gave her a beady stare with his one good eye. 'Are ye a pet?'

'No,' said Lu. 'Are you?'

Pew sneezed in horror.

'No! I be wild.' He said the last word with pride.

'So am I,' said Lu who wasn't sure what wild was, but it sounded good. 'So, what now? I don't like this.'

She meant the harbour with its open space and activity. Even in the dark it was far too wide. Lu felt very tiny and very exposed.

'Come to me ship,' said Pew.

'Ship?'

'It's a big home which moves with the waves.'

Lu would have asked what waves were but being snug and safe was more important.

'Is there a nest?'

'Lots of nests,' coughed Pew. 'Lots of rats as well.'

Now, it really isn't a good idea for young Bigs to run off with strangers, day or night. It isn't wise for rittens to go off with strange rats, either. In fact Lu would have been better off waiting where she was for help. But there are no such things as rat police, rat teachers, rat bus drivers or anyone else who looks after youngsters and makes sure they get home. So Lu had to make the best of it. Now she was calm she had time to notice that Pew not only couldn't see very well, he was also fat and slow. As he scuttled back to the ship he moved with a limp. Lu, who was slim and speedy, thought she could run if things went wrong.

Pew slunk his way across the harbour.

Mysterious sounds and smells came to Lu; salt and spices, wet wood, meat, fish, bananas and Bigs who shouted and clanked things and dragged heavy boxes along the ground. The stone underfoot was slippy and covered in green slime. She went up and down steps, climbed through metal rungs, slipped under gangplanks and ran-ran-ran whenever there was nowhere to hide. Pew was easy to follow because of his smell.

He climbed onto a mooring bollard which had a thick rope wrapped around it.

'Up here,' he said and waddled up the rope.

It stretched over a dark space. Lu could hear and smell the water beneath. It was deep. She used the rope like a bridge, holding on with her clever little fingers and toes. Her tail stuck out to keep her steady but she still wobbled.

The rope curved up and soon Lu was using her claws to climb. Then she found wood. It was the hull of the ship; it was smooth and the planks were tightly fixed together. Pew disappeared through a scupper (a drainage gap) and she followed.

The old rat led her across the deck and down a hole. Lu relaxed. Her whiskers told her she was somewhere tight and sheltered. It was very dark as well, which she liked.

'This is me ship,' said Pew proudly.

'It does move!' said Lu who felt the slow rocking in her whole body.

Lu suddenly realised how sleepy she felt. It was almost dawn and she had been up all night. She yawned. Outside things were getting louder. The Bigs were working faster. There was more thumping and shouting outside.

A Big shouted, 'The wind is good. Sail off!'

Neither of the rats could understand Big speak. They ignored it.

'Me ship be a great ship,' said Pew, once the booming died away. 'I will show ye all of her.'

But Lu wasn't listening. She sniff-sniffed. There was a familiar smell.

'Rip?' she said as a brown face looked down through the hole in the deck. 'Rip!'

'I came for you. Oof!' Rip said as Preen pushed her own pointed nose through the narrow gap.

'Me too!' said the little grey rat. 'We found a way out of our home. We followed your scent. We can take you back to the nest. I was scared but Rip was brave. She made me come.'

'Move quick,' said Rip. 'Go, go! The Bigs are here, lots of them.'

'Thank you!' said Lu. 'Thank you, thank you!'

She reached up to the hole, stretching her body long and thin. A bell was ringing and dozens of giant feet paced across the deck and pier. The Bigs were busy and full of purpose. They called to each other as they unwound ropes and flung them from shore to ship.

A Big shouted: 'Anchor up!'

On a lower deck, a group were bent over long poles that stuck out from a great wheel called a capstan. They pushed, the wheel turned and drew a chain out from the water.

Lu was on the weather deck. She scurried to where the long rope had been before but in the time it had taken the rats to scurry across the open space, a sailor had hauled it up.

'That was our way in and out!' said Rip.

A Big shouted, 'Cast off!'

The sails came down and pulled tight. The ship started to move away from the landing.

'Where do we go?' squeaked Preen.

'Down!' said Rip. Her claws scrabbled at the wooden planks but the bowed sides of the ship were too difficult to descend. The gap between land and ship grew every second. To the rats, with their poor eyesight, the drop seemed to go on forever. They balanced on the edge, heads bobbing up and down.

'Jump!' said Lu. She tensed and gathered her strength.

If she had made the leap, her sisters might have followed and their story would have been very different. But instead... she felt something grab her tail.

'No!'

It was Pew. He held on with both paws.

'Let go!' said Lu.

'Don't leave,' he said. 'Ye be me new friend. I need a friend.'

'Get off!' Lu felt Pew's grip weaken and her tail slipped loose.

It was too late. The ship was leaving the harbour, its tall masts creaking and the sails full of wind.

Lu turned on Pew.

'You mean rat!' she squeaked. 'You tricked me!'

'No,' he cringed. 'I want to help ye.'

'You bad rat! I will bite you hard!'

'Don't bite me!'

'Please don't bite him,' said Rip. 'You could get ill.'

Preen gazed forlornly at the shore.

'That was our last chance,' she said. 'What will we do now?'

Lu looked at Rip but she had no answer.

'What will Mum Rat think?' was all she said. 'She won't know where we are.'

Chapter 3: All at Sea

Rats are practical creatures. A young human might spend days, weeks or even years feeling homesick and missing their parents. In fact, there was a little girl on the ship doing just that at the same time the sisters were trying to work out what to do next. But rats do not have the luxury of time to mourn. And though Lu missed her Mum Rat and her brothers, at least she had her sisters – and a new 'friend'.

'I has things to do,' said Pew. 'Then it be time for sleep.'

'I know,' said Lu, who yawned.

'Can I stay with ye when I be done?'

'No,' said Rip. 'Leave us.'

Pew wilted.

'I will find ye soon,' said Pew. Then he was gone.

The three rittens were tired. They were worn out with fright and running, so they snuggled up together. Lu put her forehead against the floor, curled her tail around herself and fell asleep. Rip rested her chin on Lu's back and Preen snuggled under Rip's leg.

Pew came back at sundown. Like all rats, he was most active at dawn and dusk. He woke Lu by walking over her back.

'Hey!' Lu squeaked.

'Oops,' said Pew. 'Good day. I told the ship rats ye be here. Come and meet them.'

'First you tell us how to get home,' said Rip.

'Or we will scratch you,' said Preen.

'Please don't scratch me!' Pew said, miserably.

'We won't scratch him,' said Rip.

'We might,' muttered Lu.

'The ship goes back,' said Pew. 'It moves on the sea from place to place but it will go back to yer port.'

'When?' said Rip.

Pew made a rat shrug which is done with the toss of the head.

'Some day.'

'Till then, this is home,' said Lu. '*Kree*?'

'*Kree*,' said the other rats. And with that, all blame was put aside. Neither Rip nor Preen condemned Lu for the situation. They didn't forgive her because they didn't have to. And Lu did not feel angry or bitter at Pew.

Pew cheered up.

'Come meet the rats on me ship. This way.'

He guided the sisters through the hidden parts of the vessel. There was room between the decks, little rat runs, forgotten spaces and hidey-places running from the bilge at the bottom of the ship to the quarter deck at the top. Pew knew them all.

He took them to the orlop. This was the heart of the rat's floating home, below the level of the sea. It was a shallow deck above the hold where the sailors stored their ropes. Bigs didn't use it very often.

Lu and her sisters wriggled their way over and around the coiled lines. They were wary. They could smell other rats.

'Who goes there?'

The question came from a very large rat who squatted on the tallest coil of rope.

'Arr, it be Pew and me three friends, sir.'

'You don't have any friends, Pew,' said the big rat. 'Who are these new rats and where are they from?'

'Land, sir.'

'And why are they here?'

Lu did not want to sniff-sniff this new rat, even though it was impolite to refuse. He was big but in a totally different way to Pew who was baggy and soft. This rat was tough and made of muscle. Lu could tell from his smell he was dangerous. She flicked her ears. Dozens of other rats surrounded them, their noses twitching. She made herself small.

Pew went to sniff-sniff the big buck but the new rat put a pink paw on Pew's face and pushed him away, which was as rude as barging past a gentleman who has offered to shake hands.

'I led them to me ship, sir,' said Pew.

'It is not your ship,' said the big rat. 'It is my ship. I am the Skip.'

'I was Skip once,' muttered Pew.

'Not now, though. You do not have the Curl. You are just old and fat and you stink.'

'Who are you?' asked Lu, bravely.

'I am Black Spot. I am the Skip of this ship. This is the Curl which proves it.'

Black Spot gestured to a scrap of cloth next to him. It was a piece of gold brocade bent into a loop.

'To be Skip you must be the strongest rat. I beat Pew. I even beat the Bigs. This is my proof. I was in the den of the Big Skip. I saw this shine. I stole it. It is mine now and so is the ship. You see?'

'Yes,' said Preen.

'You say 'yes, *sir*',' said Black Spot, showing his long, strong yellow teeth.

'What is a Skip?' Lu said quietly.

'Don't ask daft things,' said Rip. 'Skip means he's boss rat. He's in charge.'

'Who am I?' said Black Spot.

'You are the Skip, sir,' said all three sisters.

'Come close, let me see you.'

Lu, Preen and Rip climbed the coil of rope. Black Spot checked them from nose to tail. Lu quivered as he inspected her.

'Pew, you fool,' said Black Spot. 'You brought pets here!'

The circle of black and brown rats all flinched at his anger.

'You smell of Bigs.'

This was because of the stuffing Mum Rat had pulled loose from a chair to use in their home nest. It came from a seat cushion which was so old and well used it had begun to take on the shape of the office manager's bum.

'Pets spend time with Bigs. They do what Bigs want. Pets are not real rats. They are not like us,' said Black Spot. 'They are soft and they like Bigs. We all know Bigs are bad, so we can't trust pets, too.'

'We are not like that,' Lu insisted.

Black Spot's whiskers bristled.

'Pew, do you not see what you have done? No, of course not. You only have one eye,' he said, spitefully. 'They are pets. This one is too pale. No wild rat looks like this.'

'My Mum Rat told us not to go near Bigs,' said Lu. She missed her mother with a hard, sudden pain.

'Your Dad must have been a pet then,' said Black Spot.

'So what if he was?' said Rip. She ground her teeth.

'So you have no place here,' said Black Spot. 'A ship can hold some rats but not all of us. We need food and nests to hide in. There is no room for lots of us. There is no room for weak pets who will get caught and cause us strife.'

'There is no place for us to go,' said Preen.

'No,' said Black Spot. 'There is not. We will throw you off the ship. You will fall in the sea and drown. Catch them!' he ordered the watching circle of rats. The ship rats leaped at the land rats. Suddenly there were teeth and claws everywhere. Preen squealed.

'Don't tear my fur!'

Rip went to her rescue.

Lu fought, kicking and scratching. She bit a strange rat and he shrieked. She wriggled out from the pile of struggling rodents.

'Skip, sir!' she said, thinking quickly. 'Stop! We know you are the boss rat because you have the Curl as proof. What proof would we need to show we are wild, not pets?'

Black Spot, who hadn't moved during the flurry, sniffed once. Everyone stopped fighting and went still. This scared Lu even more. How could Black Spot command a gang of rough ship rats with a single snort? What terror must they feel for their Skip?

'Ah,' he said. 'Proof. I could set you a test. You will try and I will watch. You will fail and I will laugh. Why not?'

Lu sensed a trap.

'What test?'

'A test of things a wild rat is and things wild rats must do. Wild rats can sneak, steal, scrap, swim and scale. You must show me you can do these things. Then you can stay.'

'Swim where?' said Preen who was a bit scared of water and wanted to keep her fur just so.

'Fight who?' said Rip who was too peaceful to enjoy battle.

'Sneak where? Steal what?' sneered Black Spot. 'I choose your test. There will be one each day for five days. If you fail you go in the sea. Do you say yes?'

'Don't,' warned Rip, who did not trust Black Spot.

But Lu had a plan. It relied on *kree*, on rat honour. Rats cheat and thieve, sometimes even from each other, but they are social animals and have to live together, whatever their argument. So they agree to forgive and forget as long as they survive the dispute. And they tend to keep their word. Lu hoped the other ship rats would remember *kree* even if Black Spot did not.

'If we show you we three can sneak, steal, scrap, swim and scale you will see we are wild?' said Lu, carefully. 'Sir?'

'Yes.'

'*Kree*?'

'*Kree*, pet.'

'Done,' said Lu. She sniffed noses with Black Spot to seal the deal. Preen and Rip chittered with nerves.

'Leave,' said Black Spot.

'Come on Pew,' said Lu. 'Show us where to make a nest.'

Pew sneezed.

'This is not good,' said Rip as they left the orlop and dropped into the hold. Pew showed them a place between two packing crates. The sisters squeezed in. They found something even better than a hidden place between two boxes: one of the crates had holes drilled in it. They were just big enough for the rittens to pass through.

'I can't come in!' said Pew when he tried to follow.

'Good,' said Preen who, unlike Lu, was not sure she forgave the old rat just yet.

'Oh,' said Pew. 'You are mean to me.' Then he excused himself and went elsewhere.

The sisters found themselves in a big box full of straw. There was a soft cloth under their feet that covered something lumpy and warm. This was a luxurious place to snooze. They started cleaning themselves, brushing their paws over their ears. Lu found washing helped her think.

'We can't do all these tests!' said Preen. 'We are small. This is our first time out of our home.'

'We don't all have to do the tests,' said Lu, cunningly. 'Black Spot did not say we *each* should do five tests. He said we *three* should do five tests. I could sneak, you could steal, and Rip could climb. You see?'

'I do see,' said Rip. 'We do what we do best. That's smart.'

'What does scale mean?' said Lu.

'It means climb,' said Rip.

'Oh,' said Lu, who knew she was rather clumsy. 'Rat-bum.'

The sisters piled on top of each other and went to sleep.

Chapter 4: The Small Big

As sharp as rats can be, even they make mistakes, especially when they are new to the world. So if the crate was surprisingly spacious and easy to get into the rats didn't question it. If the air in the crate was unusually warm, they didn't notice it. They were just glad to be safe and dry.

It came as quite a shock when the warm thing they were sleeping on, which moved up and down very gently, suddenly rolled over and sat up.

'Meep!' squeaked Preen.

'Eeep!' squeaked Rip.

'Peep!' squeaked Lu. They buried themselves in the straw.

The thing in the crate stretched its huge arms. It blew air out of its mouth. Then it made a loud noise the rats couldn't understand and which seemed to go on forever. To another Big, though, it would have sounded like this (as long as they could speak Swedish): 'Oh, I'm so cramped.'

Lu risked poking her nose out of the straw.

'It's a girl Big!' said the white rat.

The Big heard rustling.

'I bet that's mice,' she said. Lu shrank back, but the girl kept making noises. 'It's fine. I'm not scared. I had a pet mouse once. I bet you aren't so different from him. I used to talk to him when I was lonely. He was good at listening and never talked back – that meant he didn't give me any bad advice. Do you mind if I chat to you?'

Lu, of course, couldn't understand a word of this but the Big didn't sound angry and wasn't moving so she felt safe for now.

'Would you like some cheese?' the girl rummaged around. Lu smelled something deliciously savoury. She crept out from the straw. Her whiskers told her she was alone - Preen and Rip had fled. They wanted nothing to do with the Big.

The girl did exactly the right thing for making friends with a small animal. She sat still and waited with a treat on the palm of her hand.

Lu came closer. She put her paws on the hand. The girl let out a little gasp but she didn't jerk away.

Very delicately, Lu picked up the cheese and nibbled it. Her long tail touched the girl's arm.

'You are too big to be a mouse,' said the girl in a quavering voice. 'And your tail is bald. But you haven't bitten me yet. You must be a nice creature.'

Lu sniffed for more cheese. Her tickling whiskers made the girl laugh.

'No more, sorry. I haven't much food. I have to save it. I'm posting myself to Jamaica, you see.'

Lu sat on her haunches and cleaned her face. She felt quite comfortable with this Big.

'My name is Runa. I live in Millardia in Sweden. I suppose you're wondering why I'm posting myself across the ocean?' Runa said to Lu, who wasn't. The ritten was really wondering if there was more cheese.

'I'll tell you why. My father is a very important man. He has gone to the New World to see if he can buy land. My mother died when I was little so my father left me with a governess.

'I hate her. The governess, I mean, not my mother. She's cruel. She hits me with a long stick when I get my sums wrong, which is all the time. She smacks me on my hands in German and French lessons and on my backside if she sees me in the corridor. She doesn't let me speak except to answer questions. If she hears my voice when I'm not in a lesson, she tells the maids to feed me nothing but dry bread. I wrote to father but I think she burns the letters he writes back to me.

'Father left me some money. I was going to spend it on food, clothes and sensible things but then I thought the governess would catch me when I came back to the house and take any food away from me. So I decided to leave forever.

'I arranged for a packing crate to be sent to the house. I put everything I thought I'd need in it. I made sure there were air holes. I think you used them as a door. Then Astrid, my friend and favourite maid, sealed me in and sent me off. I went by coach to Vernaya Port and then I was loaded onto this ship.

'I'm going to find my father.'

Lu butted the Big girl with her nose.

'No, no more cheese for you, little one. I have scarcely enough for me. Do come back, though. It's good to have company.'

Lu decided it was time to go.

She could tell it was dawn and she was hungry. The scrap of cheese had only made her stomach growl.

Pew and her two sisters were outside.

'What do we eat?' Lu said after a greeting sniff-sniff.

'There be hard tack, salt beef, dry peas, sour milk, oats and things,' said Pew.

'Yum,' said Preen. She did not sound enthusiastic.

'I will show ye where it be.'

Pew set off with a limping waddle. He led them to the part of the hold that held the food supplies. The rats found themselves looking up the looming sides of a barrel.

'I smell it,' said Rip. 'Oats.'

They nosed their way around the base but there was no way in. The wood was set tight together and bound by iron rings. They stretched up but the barrel was too tall.

'Ye must go in through the top,' said Pew.

That didn't seem like a good idea to Lu.

'Why us?'

'I be old. I can't drop. If I fall I will break.'

Lu worked out what he meant. The sides of the barrel were too steep to climb. There was nowhere to get her claws in. The obvious way to get up was to climb the bulkhead, a dividing wall made of planks braced with beams of wood. From there a clever rat could use the beams as a ladder then spring onto the barrel lid. But to Lu, with her bad eyes, it would have felt like skydiving through cloud with no way to know where she would land. She did not fancy leaping into nothing.

'Er, no thanks,' said Preen.

'Bad plan,' said Rip.

Lu looked at Pew.

'This is why you brought me here,' she said. 'To bring you food.'

Pew smelled of shame.

'Ye be young,' he said. 'I be weak and half blind. I need help. Black Spot be strong but ship rats bring him food and stash it by his throne for him to eat. It ain't fair. I hate him.'

Lu was shocked. Because of *kree*, it was very unusual for rats to bear a grudge. Black Spot must have done something terrible to Pew.

'Why don't you just leave?' said Preen.

'I were born on this ship. She be my home. Ye want to go back to yer home and I want to stay in mine, see?'

Pew looked sad and old.

Lu chirruped her annoyance.

'Fine, I'll go,' she said.

She started to haul herself up the bulkhead. She put her back feet down flat on each beam, reached to the next and pulled herself up. It was tough. She drew herself long and narrow as she stretched on tiptoe. She had to press tight to the wall to avoid teetering. She used her whippy tail for balance.

Slowly, she made her way to the top. Lu risked looking over her shoulder as she clung to the wood. It was a long way down.

'Meep!' she shouted.

'Peep!' someone answered from far below.

And then… she fell. The world went up as she went down. Then she landed - plop - on the barrel deck.

She shook herself to clear her jangling head.

'Are you all right, Lu?' said Rip.

'I can't climb,' said Lu, sadly.

'I'll do it,' said Rip. Lu watched her sister clamber up the wall and on to the top of the barrel. It was partly open – which was why they could smell the oats. It was easy to sneak under the lid.

Rip stood on the oats and kicked with her back legs, sending them into the air. They rained down on the waiting rats. Lu was so hungry she forgot to be upset. She stuck her snoot into the food and started munching.

Rip leaped from the barrel to the floor. Imagine a man leaping from a four-floor building. He would go splat! But Rip landed just fine.

'Thanks!' Pew said, chewing away.

'Don't be sad you can't climb, Lu,' said Rip. The sisters hid under a canvas to eat.

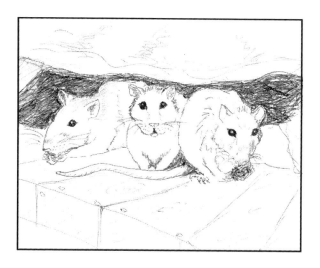

They ate breakfast until their bellies bulged. Then they explored the vessel, or at least the parts where no Bigs were working.

The *Hydromyst* wasn't like the wallowing galleons of earlier times. It was a fat-bellied trader called a *fluyt*, a full-rigged ship with three mighty masts bearing big sails. It had a weather deck that was open to the sky, a forecastle at the front and quarterdeck at the back that held the Captain's cabin.

The main deck was where most of the sailors slept and lived. Below that was the orlop and then the hold, which was the biggest space on board. Even further down was the bilge where stagnant water gathered and had to be pumped out.

Built by Dutch shipwrights, it was a handsome vessel made to carry huge amounts of cargo. Despite that, it rode the waves like a sledge rides snow. Its crew, who were all Dutch, were very proud of her for the most part, aside from a handful of untrustworthy sorts who will come into the story later.

Their Captain was a tall man who wore a fine jacket and styled his hair with wax. He stood very straight and had no patience for sloppiness. His men had grog rations but drunkenness was forbidden on his ship, although some of the more rascally sailors stole extra shares and hid liquor around their bunks.

Of the *Myst's* decks, the weather and main deck were the busiest, with the sailors on the day watch moving up and down the rigging, tightening and slackening lines, trimming the sails, painting the wood, scrubbing the planks and doing a dozen more things which meant nothing to the rats.

Lu, who hid in the shadows, squinted up at the main mast. It went up further than she could see. She could hear cloth flapping and waves shushing.

'That is a long climb,' said someone behind them. Preen went rigid. None of them had seen this rat approach. The new rat sniff-sniffed them, one by one.

'I am Sleek,' she told them. 'Black Spot wants me to fetch you. He will not leave his throne. Come with me.'

The three sisters had no choice. They followed Sleek.

Chapter 5: The First Test

Sleek escorted them back through the ship.

On the main deck, the rest of the crew worked or snoozed, depending on their shift.

The rats skirted round them and found their way into the orlop.

Black Spot sat on his throne of coiled rope.

A doe rat ran up with something in her mouth. It was a scrap of salt meat. She dropped it at his feet and scuttled off.

'I have your first test,' he said, chewing. 'First you must sneak.'

'I will do it,' Lu volunteered. Beside her, Pew was shivering. 'Sir,' she added.

'You will all do it,' said Black Spot.

'No, sir,' said Lu, bravely. 'You said we three should take the tests but you did not say all of us should do all of them. It should be enough that we can do the tests as a team.'

Black Spot glowered. Some rats can frown and he was one of them. Rip flinched.

'You made the rules and set them,' Lu pressed, though secretly her back legs were shaking. She made her voice firm.

'You swore by *kree*.'

'Ye did,' said Pew, faintly. 'And all the rats saw.'

Black Spot hissed. Hissing is the worst noise a rat can make. It's the sound of terrible fear or murderous rage.

'Fine,' said Black Spot, spitefully. 'If we are to play by the rules then you should do two tests, for I said five days and five tests and you have been here more than a day. You must sneak and steal at the same time.'

'I will,' said Lu.

'But you are white!' squeaked Preen. 'You will be seen. I am grey so I will not be seen.'

'Let me do this,' said Rip. 'I was born first so I should go first.'

'I am the small one,' said Lu. 'So I can sneak and steal.' She did not wait for her sisters to argue. 'What should I do?'

'You must go to the bunks. Find the sleeping Big with the long face fur. He is most proud of this fur and strokes it often. He grooms it each day with a long thing with teeth, as his are blunt. It is called a comb. You must steal his comb and bring it to me.'

Lu blinked. This shouldn't be too hard, she thought.

'He must not wake and no Big must see you,' said Black Spot. 'I will have eyes on you. Now go.'

The three sisters stalked away, followed by Pew and Sleek.

'He scared me so much I peed a bit,' said Preen.

'He scared me so much I did a poo,' said Pew. The sisters edged away from him.

'Right,' said Lu. 'I'll go before the Big with the fur wakes.'

'Good luck,' said Rip.

'Be safe,' said Preen. They touched noses.

Lu wriggled up a vent and came out on the main deck where the bunks, the capstan and the galley were housed, together with a few cabins for the ship's mates and other high-ranking sailors.

Lu could smell someone cooking a bacon breakfast.

She ran as swift as a whisper along the hull, always trying to keep under cover. She used bunks, trunks and baggage to hide behind. Every so often she peered up. No one noticed the pale little rat face with rippling whiskers.

She hunted. Finally she spotted a man lying in a bunk. He was sleeping bare-chested with his mouth open. A great, red bushy beard and moustache fluttered as he breathed.

'That's him, ' Lu said to herself.

Lu wove her way to his bunk and slipped into his boot. She was just in time. Two sailors walked past laughing at a joke. It was the Second Mate and a deck hand and they were both a bit tipsy.

The comb was nowhere to be seen. Lu snuffed around the sailor's bags and belongings but she couldn't find it.

Lu waited until the coast was clear and ventured up the side of the bunk. She spotted the comb, then. It was on the other side of the bunk, half out of a little bag containing soap and a tin of wax. Black Spot had not lied; this sailor definitely took pride in his face fur.

Lu hid under a fold of the thin, grey ship's blanket. She could feel the sailor's slow, sleepy heartbeat. Her own heart was going at a gallop.

Unfortunately, this sailor was large - even for a Big - and the bunk was both narrow and short. He spilled over the edges. The only way to reach the bag was across him.

'Not fair,' Lu said. She realised Black Spot had made the challenge as hard as possible.

If Lu ran over the sleeping sailor he might wake up and she would fail. But if she didn't, Black Spot would force Rip and Preen into the sea.

Gingerly, Lu put a little pink paw on the sailor's arm. He grunted and she shot back under the blanket.

After a while, he hadn't moved or woken so she tried again. She trod lightly as she travelled up his arm and over his chest. Someone walked past and she went still. Her eyes were the only things that moved. They followed three sailors as they strolled along the rolling deck. The men were busy speaking in Dutch. They didn't notice little Lu crouched on their colleague's chest.

Lu whisked across the rest of the sailor's belly and found the bag. She closed her teeth around the comb.

Now came the really difficult bit.

All the fur on Lu's body prickled as she dragged the comb away from the wall. It was awkward. It was as long as her and impossible to lift entirely so Lu had to keep one end on the sailor. Rats can bite through concrete but they are not equipped to carry things over long distances. They don't have soft mouths like gun dogs or pouches in their cheeks like hamsters. So Lu struggled, juggling the comb between her jaws and paws. The edge poked into the bearded sailor's belly. He grumbled.

Lu ran for it. She scrambled up his torso.

The comb went through the sailor's curly chest fur, brushing it into neat stripes. It must have tickled because he laughed and slapped his hand against his skin. It missed Lu by a hair.

She hopped off the sailor to the floor where she hid under the bunk.

Her sides were heaving.

She'd done it!

And it was just in time because suddenly a bell started ringing and everything was commotion. The bearded sailor woke. Lu saw his feet swing down to the deck.

'What is it?' he said. To Lu it sounded like roaring.

'A stowaway in the hold,' said another sailor. 'The Bosun heard rats squeaking and went to look. He found someone.'

'Yuck, rats,' said the bearded sailor. 'I dreamed one was on my chest. We should get a ship's cat.'

Then they were gone.

Lu came out. She pulled the comb across to a hole in the deck and dropped it before following it down to the orlop.

Black Spot and a circle of adult rats were waiting for her.

'I can sneak and I can steal,' said Lu. 'Here is the proof.' She left the comb at his feet.

Black Spot sniffed.

'Huh,' he said. 'You had good luck. The next time you might not.' He picked up the comb and placed it next to the Curl.

Lu beat a retreat.

Rip and Preen found her.

'You did well,' said Rip.

'They found the Big in the box!' said Preen. 'They took it to a dark place.'

'Who cares?' said Rip. 'It's just a Big.'

The trio cuddled up. Pew sat on the outside of the pile looking mournful.

'Oh come on,' said Lu. 'We won't push you out.'

The old rat gratefully curled up with his back to them.

They slept through the rest of the day.

Chapter 6: The Second Test

At dusk, they woke. The deck bell was ringing to gather the first watch.

'I be in need of food,' said Pew, stretching. His back clicked.

The four rats went down to the hold and split up. Pew told them it was no good to go back to the oat barrel. He knew from experience it would be sealed up tight by now.

Lu went sniffing around the crates. She travelled quite far, skirting past the wide base of the main mast. The deck to the aft of the ship angled up. This part of the hold was divided into compartments full of mail and equipment. Lu ran past them. Nothing smelled tasty but there was something further on.

The whiff of food was coming from the brig.

This was a closed compartment like a little jail cell. There were two Bigs standing outside. One was the Captain and the other was the Bosun.

'Make sure someone checks her every four hours,' said the Captain.

'Some of the men are saying we should put her off, Skipper,' said the Bosun. 'They say it's bad luck to have a woman aboard.'

'Nonsense,' said the Captain. 'We can't turn back to port. We're on a schedule. Besides, she's a child, not a woman. She doesn't count.' He sighed. 'We don't know who she is or anything. Don't we have anyone on this cursed ship who speaks Swedish?'

'I'm afraid not, Skip.'

'See she doesn't starve,' said the Captain. 'And get her some boy's clothes. That might stop the superstitious chatter.'

'Aye Skip.'

The Bigs left.

Lu followed her nose. There was a gap under the brig door. She wriggled under it and pressed herself through.

Runa was sitting on the other side stuffing salt meat and bread in her mouth. She saw Lu.

'Hello!' she said, once the food went down. 'You must be my friend from the box. It's good to see you. Some of your friends were having a party outside my hiding place, which was a bit rude. They should have invited me. It's not so bad here, though. I'm used to bread and water and it's quite a relief to be out of that box. I have to say I hadn't thought enough about what would happen once I'd been in there a while. At least the sailors have given me a bucket I can use.'

Lu looked at the plate on the girl's knee.

'Oh, I see,' said Runa. She was half teasing. 'You only want me for my food. Well, if you are going to have dinner then you should earn it. My mouse learned tricks. Maybe you can too. Let's see how clever you are.' Runa pulled a piece of bread apart and offered it to Lu.

Lu wasn't sure if she wanted to get too close to the girl. Black Spot warned she would be watched. But she was so hungry...

She tiptoed to the bread. Runa lifted it up so Lu stood on her back feet and gently took the crumb from the Big's fingers. She nibbled the bread.

'That's very cute!' said Runa. 'You have cheered me up. Shall we play some more games?'

She had changed into the shorts and shirt that a sailor had flung into the brig but she still had her old clothes with her. She took a loose thread from her petticoat and wound it around a scrap of bread. Then she dangled it above Lu. The little rat stretched but couldn't reach.

Lu was determined. She scrambled up Runa's arm and onto her hand. Runa giggled at the tickling paws.

Lu tried everything she could think of to grab the dangling bread. She hung on to Runa's thumb and went upside down, using her tail as a safety rope. She fell off. She climbed up again, jumped and missed.

'Silly, clumsy ratty,' said Runa. 'You'll never do it that way. You'll have to snap the string or pull it up.'

Now rats aren't clever in all the ways we measure cleverness; they can't read books, for instance. But they are quite good at simple puzzles once they've been shown how to solve them and they do have a strong talent for nibbling. Lu put her teeth on the thread and gnawed it in frustration.

'Clever ratty!' said Runa. 'Bite-bite!'

The thread broke and the bread fell. Lu retrieved her treat.

The fact Runa told her to bite was a complete coincidence but rats are fast learners. Runa wound up the thread and repeated the trick. Every time Lu sat on her hand, Runa plucked the thread and said, 'bite-bite!'. She trained Lu to put the sound with the action, exactly like teaching a dog to sit or roll over.

Meanwhile, Lu was happy because this was a fun game; almost as fun as play fighting or exploring, and she got a tasty treat at the end of it. After a while, though, Runa ran out of bread and Lu got bored.

She allowed Runa to run a finger along her back once and then she skittered off in search of her sisters.

'Goodbye ratty,' said Runa, sadly.

Rip, Preen and Pew had made their own arrangements for dinner. Before they rested for the night, they had a discussion.

'Which of us should fight?' said Lu. 'Preen and I scrap all the time. I will do it.'

'Not you,' said Rip. 'You are too small and you need rest. Preen or I will do it.'

'Then who will swim the next day?'

Preen's big black eyes went even bigger.

'We don't know how to swim,' she said.

'We will both have a go,' said Rip. 'We will have to learn. We will train to swim before Black Spot's test. Don't fret.'

Preen looked scared. Rip and Lu groomed her fur to calm her down. Lu was worried for Preen. Her middle sister was shy and not as solid as Rip or as bouncy as Lu. Perhaps the tests would be too much for her.

They all snuggled up and went to sleep.

The ship sailed on, further from land, further from their mother.

Sleek woke them in the morning.

'Black Spot waits,' she said.

She led them to the orlop.

Black Spot didn't greet them. He sat looking regal on his throne and declared: 'You must swim.'

'What?' said Lu. 'It is time to scrap!'

'I say you must swim,' said Black Spot. 'You will go from the stem to the stern and back. Take them down to the bilge.'

Sleek led them deeper than they had ever gone before, down to the bowels of the ship. It stank of bad water, damp timbers and filth. This was the bilge. The sides sloped down to drain the water into a central well. The space was not big enough to allow a man to crawl through. The bilge water made a lake across the ribs of the ship. Jagged stones lay hidden at the bottom. They were the remains of ballast, there to keep the ship bottom-heavy so it stayed the right way up. They made the bilge treacherous.

'Swim through that?' said Preen in horror.

The scummy liquid was not just water. Strange things bobbed in it. It wasn't sewage, exactly, but it was not nice. This was all the stale liquid that leaked through the planks because, no matter how well made a ship is, water will find its way in eventually. Germs and all sorts of things grew in it.

Rats, despite their bad reputation, do not like dirt. They prefer to be clean and spend a lot of their time tending their fur. Preen was even cleaner than most. Her coat was soft and spotless. The idea of swimming through gunk made her very unhappy.

Rip was not pleased either.

'You have to jump in,' said Sleek. She sounded sorry. There were other rats watching them.

'We will go,' said Rip to Lu. 'You stay.'

She plopped into the reeking, swaying water. Preen reluctantly followed.

It was deeper than usual because the pumps were not being manned. Preen and Rip immediately sank.

For a long moment, Lu could only see ripples and then bubbles.

'Meep!' she called. 'Meeeep!'

Sleek snuffled.

Then a nose broke through the scum. Rip's head followed. She started paddling, holding her face above the surface.

Preen was still nowhere to be seen.

Pew and Sleek fidgeted. Lu ran back and forth at the water's edge.

'Preen? Preen?' she called in alarm. 'Where are you? Come up, Preen!'

Then they heard splishing and a series of disgusted squeaks.

'I-don't-like-it, I-don't-like-it, I-don't-like-it!'

It was Preen. She'd gone so far and fast under water they could barely see her. Now she moved like an otter. She left a v-shaped wake as she sped through the bilge. Her disgruntled meeping faded as she reached the far end of the ship and grew louder as she turned back.

'Yuck, yuck, yuck, yuck, yuck!'

She almost came up against Rip going the other way.

Then the pumps started.

A chain rattled and the water sucked up through hollow elm-tree tubes.

The bilge water drained away under them. This brought the two paddling rittens closer and closer to the sharp grit and stones at the bottom.

Preen kept her head. She barged into Rip and pushed her back onto the sloping deck. Her back feet were scraping something nasty by the time she pulled herself up.

The two rats hauled themselves out. They looked scrawny with their coats plastered down.

'You can swim, Preen!' said Lu.

'Yes, yes. I must wash,' said Preen, and she got down to the important business of scraping the muck off, fluffing out and smoothing her fur.

Meanwhile, a strange rat appeared. He had been put on a watch by Black Spot to check if the sisters reached the other side.

'We will tell Black Spot,' he said.

And they did.

When the strange rat delivered the news, Black Spot didn't say anything.

'They did well, Skip!' said the watch-rat.

Black Spot huffed.

He stalked up to the top of his throne with his tail held stiff with anger.

'Well done,' said Sleek, once they were away from the boss rat.

'Bleh,' said Preen as she found something nasty on her back. Lu and Pew helped her and Rip to clean off.

It was time for breakfast.

'I know where to find food,' Lu said. 'The Big feeds me.'

'No thanks,' said Rip. 'Bigs are bad news. You should not be with it.'

But Lu was stubborn. She did not want to hunt for food when she could get it easily. She scurried to the brig and found Runa.

The little girl was curled up on the floor. Lu sniffed her face. It smelled salty. Lu didn't understand tears. She nudged Runa with her nose.

'Oh,' said the little girl, wistfully. 'I'm still here. I dreamed I was back home in bed with a breakfast of buttered shrimp on toast. Pa was home in my dream.

'Oh well,' she said, more brightly. 'It's good to see you, ratty. Would you like to play? I saved you something from supper.'

She fed Lu crumbs from her fingers, and then when breakfast came she played the 'bite-bite' game with scraps of bacon fat. Lu snipped through the thread with her sharp front teeth.

'You're like a pair of scissors,' said Runa.
'No, there is no more. We've run out.'

This time Lu let the girl scratch the top of her head before she scuttled away.

Chapter 7: The Third Test

By now the ship was more than four days from port. The *Hydromyst* had sailed between England and France, past the northernmost point of Spain and was forging into the ocean. She was running swiftly, pushed by fair winds, and the Captain thought she should be due to dock in Jamaica within the month, if conditions were good.

Unfortunately, weather is not a certain thing. None of the crew knew they were two days from sailing into a terrible storm. The instruments on board showed nothing to worry about. The mercury in the barometer had not yet fallen. But the rats sensed something in the air and they huddled up close.

The strange tension did not make Black Spot any kinder.

He sent Sleek to summon them for their third test before dawn the next day. It was very early.

'Wake up,' she said to the sleeping rittens. 'Please wake.'

'Nooo,' said Preen. She was so tired she couldn't open her eyes properly.

'Black Spot wants you,' said Sleek.

'This is not a good time,' said Rip, blearily.

'I know. But Black Spot says now,' said Sleek. She did not sound happy.

Lu stretched her back into a C-shape as she yawned.

'We will go,' she said.

They wobbled and wandered down to the orlop.

Black Spot was already sitting on his throne.

'We are tired,' said Lu.

'I don't care,' said Black Spot. 'You can sneak, steal and swim. Now it is time to scrap.'

Rats fight quite often, but rarely in a serious way. Lu and Preen squabbled quite a lot in a friendly manner and it is quite usual for both male and female rats to sort out their differences or work out who is in charge by having a mock battle.

The goal of these fights is to bite your opponent on the backside while they try their best to stop you and bite your bum instead. As a consequence, fighting rats tend to stand up on their hind legs, face to face, and slap at each other to push each other over. It's a blend between boxing, wrestling and a strange game of tag. Other fights involve rats pinning down and energetically licking their opponent's fur which, at its worst, makes them go a bit bald.

Sometimes, though, things get more dangerous.

The sisters realised this would be one of the serious fights when they saw the massive rat lurking behind Black Spot.

He was easily three times the size of any of the trio.

'This is Thug,' said Black Spot. 'He will fight one of you. Who will he crush?'

The sisters twittered with worry.

'If you do not fight, you fail,' said Black Spot. 'Do you give in?'

Preen backed away. So did Rip. Lu, though, was so sleepy her brain wasn't quite working. She stood still and blinked.

All Thug had to do was rear up and smash down on her and that would be the end.

'I will not wait,' said Black Spot. 'Beat them, Thug.'

'Yes, Skip.'

Thug came at them. He was fast as well as large. Lu just had time to throw herself out of the way. He turned on her. Lu dodged. His jaws snapped shut on nothing. He whirled again and whipped Lu with his strong tail. Lu, confused, went: 'Peep!'

Thug batted her with his front paw. She fell. She was on her back. Thug stepped on her. Lu wriggled but it was no good.

'You lose,' said Black Spot. 'You lose!'

'Not yet!' came another voice and suddenly Lu could breathe again. The weight lifted. Thug was gone. Lu stood up.

Rip was fighting the big buck rat!

She moved like lightning. She scratched and bit and squeaked with rage.

'You don't hurt Lu!' she said. 'You won't hurt Preen! You can't hurt me. I will beat you!'

Lu had never seen her sister so enraged. Come to that, she'd never seen Rip fight before. She was good at it. She was all puffed up like a furious thistle.

Rip's angry attack took Thug by surprise. She nipped his nose, clawed his chest and drove him back. When he tried to reach around and bite her on the bum she lifted her back leg, twisted round and kicked him in the face.

She was so ferocious Thug turned and ran. Rip bit him just above his tail. He squealed.

'You win, you win!'

'No, Thug, fight!' said Black Spot. 'Fight them!'

'I don't want to!' said Thug.

'You must!'

But Thug was beaten. He slunk back to the Skip.

'You let me down,' Black Spot said, sniff-sniffing the trembling rat. 'Get off my throne.'

'I won!' said Rip.

'You can scrap!' said Preen.

'She did win,' said Lu to Black Spot. She didn't call him 'Skip'.

'Leave,' he hissed. 'You have one more test. You will fail. Leave now.'

The sisters went back to the hold. They were still exhausted from lack of sleep. Pew and Sleek came with them. To their surprise, so did Thug. He wasn't really hurt even though his bum throbbed a bit.

'Hi,' he said.

'Hi,' said Lu. 'No more fights, please.'

'No,' said Thug. 'Black Spot made me fight. He scares me. He is mean. I don't want to fight.'

Lu was not surprised about that, even though Thug was bigger than the Skip. Sometimes meanness is more dangerous than strength.

'He scares us too,' said Preen.

'Can we be friends?' said Thug. They all sniff-sniffed. Thug smelled humble and sorry. Of course, because of *kree,* the sisters forgave him.

With so many new friends the rat pile was warm and the three sisters slept well all day. In the evening, all six rats woke to find food. Sleek led them to the galley.

'You stand there where the Big can see you,' she said to Thug and Pew. 'Show him you are here. Then run. We will steal the food.'

It worked like a charm. The cook spotted the two big buck rats sitting on the galley floor and went mad. He threw a pan at them and chased them away. By the time he came back a big lump of bread, some cooked potatoes and a raw carrot had gone missing. The 'slush', a greasy mix of fats sailors used as butter, had rat foot and face marks in it.

'We really need a cat,' the cook said to himself.

Lu, Rip, Preen and Sleek shared the feast with Pew and Thug. Afterwards, most of the rats went to sleep. Lu couldn't settle. She was feeling confident about the last test, despite Black Spot's dire threats, but she was fidgety anyway. She walked over Pew and Thug, who did not wake up.

Sleek was the only one to open a single watchful eye that followed Lu as she left.

The little white rat hurried along to the brig.

Runa was asleep but she woke when Lu snuffled in her ear.

'Ee!' she said, sitting up. 'What a strange hello.'

Lu looked at her hopefully but Runa couldn't see her in the dark.

'I hope that was my ratty,' said the girl, 'and not one of the others. Give me a minute.'

She felt around for the lamp and set it alight.

'Oh good, it is you,' she said and squatted to talk to Lu. 'I saved you some breakfast but you never arrived. You might at least have sent me a message declining my invitation but I expect you had pressing rat business to attend to.'

By now Lu was fairly sure this Big was not going to hurt her. She climbed onto Runa's knee. She crouched as Runa's finger brushed against the top of her head.

'Oh don't fuss, so,' said Runa. 'Would you like to play the biting game?'

Lu pricked up her ears and looked alert.

Runa plucked a thread free from her discarded petticoat.

'If I keep taking cotton from my clothes they will fray,' she said. 'But we will do this one last time.' She hastily tied a loop around a hard biscuit.

Lu knew what to do even before the command came. She turned her head to snip the cord as Runa said: 'bite-bite!' She liked the words, even if she didn't understand them. They meant she would be rewarded soon.

She paused to wash her nose.

'People say rats are dirty,' said Runa. 'But you clean all the time. You are quite the lady. And you haven't bitten me once.'

When the biscuit was gone, Runa got Lu to play chase with a piece of straw. Lu pounced on it.

'You are like a little cat sometimes. Other times you are like a little dog. But mostly I think you are yourself. If I ever find my Pa and bring him home I'd like to take you too, you know. You could live in your own room with your own bed and lots of things to climb on and all the food you could ever want. I would give you good greens and berries and also boiled eggs, nuts and fish. You would get candies, if you were good, but only sometimes. You would never have to eat hard biscuit again.'

There was a bang on the door. Two red-rimmed eyes peered through the bars.

'Who are you talking to in there, girl?' The drunken sailor frowned.

By now, the sailors and Runa had found enough common words between Swedish and Dutch to say simple things. Fortunately, her horrible governess had forced her to learn a bit of German, which had a lot in common with Dutch. However, the conversation was still very one-way.

'Sorry?' said Runa.

This sailor was one of the rascally ones sneaking extra rations of grog. He didn't like Runa being on board but he liked being sent down to the hold because it gave him an excuse to help himself to the ship's supply of booze.

Lu could smell it sweating through him. She ran through the legs of the Second Mate who was coming to meet his friend.

'Yuck, a rat,' he said. 'Rats are disgusting. We need a cat.' He wobbled a bit as the ship rocked. 'Curse these waves. Pass me that.'

His friend, the drunken sailor, burped.

'Rats are filthy, evil things. They bite babies and spread disease,' he said.

'They are as welcome on board as her and her grubby boy clothes,' said the Second Mate, speaking too quickly for Runa to follow. 'Rats and little girls should not be on ships. If I had my way they would all go overboard.'

The drunken sailor laughed.

Lu dashed back to the huddle of sleeping rats. She nosed her way in and closed her eyes.

Chapter 8: Storm Brewing

The waves were choppy and the wind blustered around the ship. The rats went about their day in a jumpy but subdued mood. They foraged, napped and spent the rest of the time creeping about as though the sky was going to fall on their heads. It wasn't just the three sisters who felt it. All the rats on the ship were uncomfortable. They had static electricity in their whiskers. Dark clouds were boiling on the horizon by the time a sailor rang six bells. The humans couldn't smell the storm but they were worried too. The Captain pored over his charts. The Bosun ordered his men to rest in case they were needed later. The First Mate told the Second Mate to keep a watch on the weather. The Second Mate sipped his grog.

Down in the rat run, Sleek nudged Lu awake.

'Hey,' she said.

'Yes?'

'We need to talk. Come with me.'

Lu yawned, her mouth snapping shut like a pink trap. She pat-pittered after the older doe.

Sleek glanced around.

'Have a care,' she said. 'You smell of Big. If Black Spot finds out you will be thrown off the ship. He won't care if you can sneak, swim or scrap. Splash! You will be gone.'

'I will stay far from Bigs,' said Lu.

'Black Spot is bad news.'

'I know.'

'You don't know all of it,' said Sleek, shivering. 'He is bad, bad news. He woke you too soon for the fight. He made Preen swim in a foul place when you thought you would have to fight. He knew what time the pumps would start. When you stole the comb he made us 'meep!' so the Bigs would find the one in the box and wake up the Big with the face fur. The tests are not fair.'

'I thought that too,' said Lu.

'Lu, do you know why Pew hates him so much?'

'Pew was Skip. Then Black Spot beat him.'

'It's worse than that. Yes, Black Spot beat Pew. He knew he'd won. That should have been it. But then he took Pew's eye out for fun,' said Sleek. 'He broke *kree*.'

'I will stay safe,' said Lu.

'Good, let's rest.'

The day crawled by. Lu dozed, searched for food and dozed again. Waiting was hard. Black Spot was taking his time.

'I wish the test would start,' said Lu to Preen. 'I don't like this.'

She groomed nervously.

'Don't pull your fur out!' said Preen.

By now the waves were lashing at the ship. It had started raining. Everyone on board could hear drops hammering on the weather deck. The Captain pulled more men in to run the bilge pumps and get rid of the water.

Lu didn't know what to do with herself.

The bell rang eight times, marking 8pm. It was getting dark. Surely Black Spot would not keep her waiting much longer?

Finally, although she knew she shouldn't, Lu went down to the hold.

What harm could one last visit to Runa do? After tonight, Lu and her sisters would be accepted as wild rats, but until then why shouldn't she play and have treats?

She set off.

She did not know she was not alone. Another rat followed her silently.

Runa was huddled in a corner. The rocking wasn't as bad this deep in the ship but it was enough to scare a girl who had never been to sea before.

'Hello ratty,' she whispered when she saw Lu. 'I keep trying to pretend I'm on the rocking chair in my Mama's room but it's no good.

'I don't want to moan at you, ratty, but I am very afraid we are going to die.'

Lu crept closer.

'I don't have any food, sorry,' said Runa. 'The sailors are all rather busy keeping this tub afloat so I'm sure I can do without dinner just fine. Besides, I might be sick.'

Lu sidled along the brig wall until she was just out of reaching distance. She looked at Runa.

'I think we've made good friends,' said Runa. 'I would like us to shake hands in case we don't make it.'

She laid her hand, palm up, on the floor.

Lu stepped on it.

Runa gasped with pleased surprise. Slowly, she lifted Lu up.

The rat made a *wuppa-wuppa* sound of shock as she glided into the air. Lu felt like she'd left most of her body back on the deck. Then Runa cupped her hands and held Lu close to her chest.

Lu relaxed. It reminded her of being back in the home nest with Mum Rat. She bruxed, grinding her teeth. It's the nearest thing a rat can do to purring.

'Thank you for coming to see me, ratty,' said Runa. A big tear plopped onto Lu's fur, followed by another. The girl sniffed and put Lu down so she could wipe her nose. 'I'm being silly. You should go and find your supper. Go on, shoo.'

Runa gave her a little wave.

Lu scampered away.

One gleaming eye watched her go. The hidden rat uncurled from the shadows and travelled to the orlop. Black Spot would be interested in this news...

Chapter 9: The Final Test

Lu reunited with her sisters who had built up a stash of grain behind a bulkhead. They were gobbling up the food when Sleek appeared.

'Come quick,' she said. 'Black Spot wants you!'

The three sisters followed her trailing tail. When they got to the orlop it was obvious every rat that could be there was sitting among the ropes. There were old ones, young ones, rats with patchy fur, rats that shone like polished oak, rats with long tails, rats with short tails, rats with blotchy tails, rats with nimble paws, rats with stumps, rats with long sharp noses and rats with round faces. There were even mother rats with tiny rittens. They all sat watching.

Black Spot was on his rope throne. The Curl was sitting next to him as a badge of honour.

'Do I climb now?' said Lu.

'Climb? Climb? No, you will fall,' said Black Spot. He reared up and all the rats quailed. 'This is a pet!' he hissed.

'No she is not,' said Rip.

'You lie!' said Preen.

'I have proof,' said Black Spot. 'A rat saw you.'

Lu looked at Sleek. The doe was shaking. She looked at Thug. He didn't seem to know what was going on. Then she smelled a ripe smell. It was Pew.

He limped forward and looked at her with his one good eye.

'Yarr. I saw the Big pick her up and hold her close,' he said.

Lu was too horrified to say anything.

'Pew, she is your friend!' said Preen.

'I know. Trust me,' said Pew, quietly.

'Why should we trust you now?' said Preen.

'Don't bite me,' Pew cringed.

'No one will bite you,' said Rip in disgust. 'You would taste too bad.'

'Why can't I spend time with a Big?' Lu found her voice. Her squeak sounded thin and weak. 'Why can't I play and eat with them? Why do you hate Bigs? My Big is just a small Big.'

'Bigs hunt us, they hurt us and they trap us,' said Black Spot. 'They spoil our food and make us sick. You can't be friends with a Big. Bigs kill rats. They hate us. They want us all dead and gone. Now I want you gone too!'

Black Spot leaped at Lu, gnashing his teeth.

Lu ran, her tail out behind her like a banner.

'Get her!' Black Spot ordered.

The other rats milled around. They weren't particularly bloodthirsty. Most of them only did what Black Spot said because they were afraid of him. They had nothing against Lu or her two sisters. But Black Spot had left his throne for the first time in a long time. The sight of him chasing the little white rat woke something in them that was driven by fear and habit. They followed. Rip, Preen, Thug and Sleek went with them.

In a few seconds only one rat was left: Pew.

He sniffed, sneezed and started to climb Black Spot's empty throne.

The ship was pitching wildly. Lu and her sisters slid to and fro across the deck as they tried to escape Black Spot. A tide of rats followed them. Everything was chaos. None of the rats bothered to hide as they were thrown from side to side, so the sailors saw them pouring up through the decks.

The ship's men were busy at the pumps or hurrying to secure the ship's articles and batten down the hatches of the lower decks. The Bosun was in charge and was shouting orders to quench any flames in the galley.

The First Mate and the Helmsman were both at the wheel, trying to keep the ship at the right angle to the wind and oncoming waves. It was a mighty task and it took two of them to hold the rudder.

The Captain gave firm, clear orders that kept the men calm.

The rats heard and felt a groaning shudder as the main mast pulled in its setting. The wood held firm and the ship pitched.

The Captain heard and felt it too. He realised something was wrong with the sails, which by now should have been reefed - tightly furled - and he shouted to one of the hands to open the deck hatch.

Lu, who was running out of places to flee, saw a flash of light and headed to the exit.

The other rats came close behind her.

A horde of stampeding rodents is the last thing a sailor wants to see, particularly if his ship is in trouble. The men shouted in dismay as the carpet of brown, beige and black fur parted around them.

'The rats are leaving!' moaned the drunken sailor. 'We're doomed!'

He went to find his friend, the drunken Second Mate who was, at that moment, up on the weather deck. He followed right behind Lu who bounced up stairs, sprinted along gangplanks and shimmied up ropes, all the while trying to shake off Black Spot.

She wasn't thinking about where she was going.

The big buck rat was gaining on her. She was fleet and agile but he had longer legs. Her tail was almost between his teeth as she whisked up the hatch on to the weather deck.

Up here things were even worse.

The wooden deck was slick with salt water and even the experienced sailors were staggering as the *Hydromyst* yawed to the side.

Some of them were trying hurriedly to tie on to a railing and make sure they were not washed overboard but their fingers were cold and stiff. They yelled to each other but their voices were lost over the howling of the wind.

The sky was a swirling horror of deep blue thunderclouds and the sea was thrashing itself into a yellow froth.

'We need to get the sails down!' the Captain shouted and looked for the Second Mate. 'We should be running bare poles!'

The Second Mate was hidden hunkered down near the forecastle. He was too wobbly to stand. His friend the drunken sailor found him.

'This is bad news!' he shouted to his friend.

The Second Mate took a swig of grog to steady his nerves, which was unfortunate as the drink was strong enough to dissolve them entirely. He was panicking. It was his watch on the upper deck and he was supposed to have kept an eye on the men trimming the sails as the wind rose but instead he'd been secretly tippling.

Now the lines attached to the masts were whipping about and the men were having a hard time climbing the rigging. Every wave threatened to throw them off and every gust of wind made it more difficult to cling on.

'The Skipper is going to kill me,' said the Second Mate, miserably.

'He might not have to,' said the drunken rogue. 'This storm might finish us off first!'

They watched as one deck hand, who was half way up the mast, lost his footing and fell. He hit the planks hard. He was lucky. His line kept him from falling into the furious sea where he would have been washed away.

'This wind is too much!' said the Second Mate. 'It is making all of us into kites! We need someone small up there, like a monkey.' He hiccupped and burped.

The drunken sailor had an evil thought. It was the kind of thought no reasonable man should ever have and perhaps if the pair of them hadn't been pickling themselves with liquor then it wouldn't have entered their brains, either.

But they were drunk, afraid and not reasonable men, so the sailor said it.

'There is someone on board who is as small as a monkey.'

'Go and fetch her,' said the Second Mate, as the Bosun himself started the climb and was blown clear of the rigging before he'd even got five feet up. 'Fetch her, give her a knife and send her up. Tell her to cut the lines. If she manages it we will have saved us all and if she washes away then it's no loss.'

Lu, of course, was still running helter-skelter across the deck. She caught no part of the conversation.

She was panting and terrified.

Nothing in her life had been this wild and noisy.

The air roared and the timbers of the ship growled as the sea pulled and pushed its planks apart. Sometimes night turned to day for a few blistering seconds as lightning struck. When that happened, the running rats and the struggling sailors were lit up in bright white.

Lu leaped up onto the balustrade of the ship and ran along it. Black Spot jumped too. They dug their claws in to stay on. Spray hit them both.

'Now you go!' said Black Spot. 'I win!'

All he had to do was bash into Lu and she would be sent spinning into the sea.

Lu looked wildly around.

There was a stay, one of the lines used to keep the masts secure. It vibrated under the pressure of the wind.

Black Spot was between Lu and the line. She jumped.

She flew over his head.

Her fingers and toes hit the rope. She climbed faster and further than she ever had before.

Even the storm wasn't loud enough to drown out Black Spot's furious hiss.

Lu went up. When she ran out of line she leaped to the next one. Now you probably wouldn't have done this because it would be like climbing a tree. Once you are in a tree there is no way down. You would be trapped. If someone is chasing you they can climb right after you and catch you. But remember, rats cannot see very well and as far as Lu was concerned, escape was anywhere Black Spot was not. She could not see the top of the mast and did not know where it ended. She just ran where the ropes took her.

Meanwhile, far below the little white rat and the angry buck, the drunken sailor had his hand tight around Runa's arm. He hauled her toward the mainmast.

She was barefoot and her boyish clothes were already soaked through from the pelting rain.

'Let me go!' she shouted in a mix of bad Dutch and angry Swedish. 'You smell of spirits!'

'Go up there,' he said. 'Cut the lines. Use this.' He handed her a knife and mimed scraping it over rope. 'Go up to the yards...' he used his hands again to describe the long straight poles the sails were attached to. 'And cut.'

Runa understood but she was frightened.

The sailor grabbed her arm again and hoisted her onto the ratline, the rope ladder the crew used to get up and down the mast.

'Go!' he roared.

Runa started to climb. Her arms and legs were shaking. She pulled herself up to the 'top', a platform about a third of the way up the mast.

There she paused.

Something dark fell past her with a scream. It was a man.

Runa couldn't carry on.

'Please let me live,' she said to the gale. 'I want to see Papa again.'

The wind replied with a blast that almost picked her off.

She clung to the ratline, her arms wrapped around the thick ropes. She closed her eyes. The ship dipped and bucked as though it was trying to throw her off.

Something soft and light landed on her shoulder. Little hands dug into her skin.

It was Lu.

In her flurry to escape, she had run all the way from one end of the ship and back again without ever touching the deck. Then she slithered down the main mast to the rope Runa hugged on to.

Lu instantly felt safer.

Black Spot hated Bigs. He wouldn't dare follow her onto Runa.

Lu snuggled into the little girl's neck.

'Ratty?' whispered Runa. 'Is that you?' Lu was shaking and half her normal size with her fur weighed down.

Black Spot stood on a spar, his teeth bared and his eyes full of hate, but he would not come closer.

'Well, I have to save you, don't I?' said Runa to Lu. Her voice was full of resolve. 'You're my friend and I have a job to do. Hold on to me.'

She inched up to grab another rope ladder and started to climb the rungs. Soon they were over the main topsail. Runa had to venture out along the yard with her toes on a footrope, her hands around a rope and the knife between her teeth. She tried to reach the fastenings.

She started sawing away at the ropes securing the sail.

Lu held on to Runa's hair, her paws making little fists.

The ropes were tough and difficult to sever.

Runa was halfway through when another gust of wind caught the sail, which billowed out.

She lost her balance and let go of the knife to grab a rail. The knife fell to the deck far below.

'Oh, now what?' said Runa to Lu. Her voice was despairing.

Lu chittered and ground her teeth with fear.

That gave Runa an idea.

'You're like a pair of scissors,' she said. 'Ratty, try this. Bite-bite!'

She pulled at the rope. Lu heard the familiar sound but she didn't understand.

'Come on ratty, bite-bite!' Runa pulled at the rope. 'It's just like our games. Come on.'

Lu sniffed.

She realised Preen and Rip were there somewhere clinging to the rigging. She could smell Thug and Sleek as well.

'Bite-bite!' said Runa.

Lu reacted automatically. She nibbled at the rope, just as Runa had trained her to do. The fibres parted.

'Good girl,' said Runa. 'Good girl!'

None of the rats understood ship rigging or physics or anything like that, but Lu suddenly knew biting was exactly what Runa wanted her to do.

She lifted her head.

'Preen, Rip,' she said. 'Do this! Bite! Tear!'

It took a moment, but then her sisters were shoulder to shoulder with her. Three pointy jaws worked. Thug and Sleek joined in and soon the tough old rope gave way.

'Bite-bite!' said Runa, pointing at the next fastening.

She looked at the sky. It was raging. Her hair was flat to her skull and her teeth were chattering as much as the rats' were. The vessel was leaning over as if it was being pushed by a huge invisible hand. If this carried on much longer it would capsize and they would all be underwater.

Lu, meanwhile, stood on her hind legs.

She squeaked to the other rats, using her whiskers, ears and every other way rats talked to each other to get their attention.

'Come up, up, up, all of you!' she said. 'Bite! Cut the ropes. Quick, quick!'

There was a moment of confusion. Not all of the rats heard and not all of them moved at once. But soon there were dozens of them hanging from the masts, spars and lines like furry pears in a very strange orchard. Rip, Preen, Sleek and Thug split up to get the message out.

The hands in the rigging, who were still struggling with the ties and lines, suddenly found themselves surrounded by busy rats.

Hundreds of teeth pressed against ropes. One by one they started snapping. The main topsail came loose and dangled on its last fastening. The wind chose that moment to stop dead.

'Look out!' shouted Runa before it fell.

Sailors ran out of the way.

The topgallant and the course sails followed. The main mast was the first to go bare. Then the rats cleared the others. The deck became a confusion of crumpled canvas. Fresh gusts of wind caught the loose sails and they flared out. One was carried away by the tempest.

The storm had less to catch now. The *Hydromyst* began to right herself. The sailors cheered.

Of course the rats didn't know which ropes were which. Nor did they stop their frantic chewing.

With the masts clear, most of the deck hands shimmied down the ladders and ratlines. But Runa, overcome with exhaustion, felt her grip on the yard weaken. One of the rats tore through the footrope and she fell, her hands sliding over the wet wood.

She didn't have time to scream before she landed.

She was lucky. One of the downed sails broke her fall.

'Stop!' shouted Lu. The other rats looked up.

She could feel through her feet that the storm had one last surprise.

'Hold on tight!' Lu squeaked.

A big wave was coming. It towered above the others like a great, blue-green cliff. It cleared the side of the boat and washed across the deck. The impact was enough to send some of the rats, including Lu, tumbling down.

Lu vanished from sight.

'All hands below deck!' called the Captain while the Bosun rang the bell. One of the last things the Captain did before ordering the hatch battened shut was scoop up the unconscious little girl and carry her below.

From now on, the only thing the crew could do was man the pumps and hope the ship could ride out the storm on its own.

Chapter 10: The Calm

At dawn the next morning, the sailors woke to a calm sea.

When the Captain and his officers ventured on to the weather deck he found scattered sails, broken spars and sections of rat-ripped rope. Some of the deck and planking had splintered and the crew had a difficult repair job on their hands. But they knew the ship was in far better shape than it would have been at the bottom of the sea.

'You're saying the rats saved us?' the Helmsman said to the Bosun.

'Aye. And the stowaway.'

The Captain frowned.

'There will be a reckoning for why the sails weren't furled as soon as the storm was spotted. Then there is the question of why the girl was sent up the rigging. How is she?'

'A bruised head, sir, but nothing much worse. She keeps asking to leave the infirmary. She is wanting after her 'white ratty',' said the Bosun.

The Captain sighed.

'I'm not sure how likely she is to find that ratty,' he said. 'I'm not sure how many survived...'

Rip and Preen weren't sure either.

They'd hidden below after the big wave and sat shivering in their own little puddles. As soon as the storm started to run out of energy they went searching belowdecks but Lu was nowhere to be found. Neither was Black Spot.

Now they ventured outside.

'Lu!' squeaked Preen. 'Lu, where are you?'

'Lu?' said Rip. 'Lu, come out.'

'I hope she has not gone in the sea,' said Thug, dolefully.

'Shh,' said Sleek.

The four rats burrowed under the fallen sails and nosed their way across the wrecked deck.

They still couldn't find her.

It was only when Preen and Rip caught a scent on one of the remaining stays they realised Lu was aloft.

They climbed the last few lines in a zigzag.

Lu was sitting right on top of the main mast. She was on her haunches, her nose turned into the wind to sniff the ocean. Her white fur was all fluffed up. She looked like a proud little figurehead.

'Hi,' said Preen. 'You can climb!'

'You are safe!' said Lu.

'So are you!' said Rip, happily.

Lu leaned down to sniff-sniff her sisters and her friends. 'I will come with you now.'

Sailors were already clearing the deck by the time the rats came down.

All the men stopped what they were doing and started to clap when they saw the furry little crew.

'Why do the Bigs hit their paws like that?' said Rip.

'I don't know,' said Lu. 'Bigs are strange.'

Of course, even though they had survived the storm, one problem had not yet been solved.

He showed up when the sisters were on the orlop helping themselves to some of the food that had been stashed there.

Black Spot was not the rat he had been the night before.

He looked exhausted. His fur was awry and his paws looked sore from the race along the rigging. He even looked a bit smaller.

'You,' he said when he saw Lu. 'Get out, pet.'

'No,' said Lu.

'Get out. Go!' Black Spot squeaked. He was puffing himself up with rage. The ship rats all looked at him to see what would happen next. 'I am Skip! I has the Curl! You do as I say! If you do not, I will pick you up and throw you off my ship!'

He stepped toward Lu.

'Not now,' said another voice. 'This ain't your ship no more. She don't has to do as ye say.'

It came from the uppermost coil of Black Spot's throne.

An old grey head popped up. A wave of odour met Lu's nose. It was Pew.

'I have the Curl,' he said. 'So I be Skip now. This is me proof.'

He lifted the golden loop in his mouth.

Black Spot stared at him in shock.

'Aye, I be smart,' said Pew. 'Ye would not leave yer throne or yer Curl but I knew ye would chase Lu if I said she were with a Big. So I told ye and ye did. I can sneak too. I went to yer throne and took the Curl from ye, like ye took it from the Big. Now I be boss rat.'

Black Spot's whiskers drooped.

He realised he'd been outwitted.

'I be the Skip once more. I say Lu can stay!' declared Pew.

'Lu can stay!' said Sleek.

'Lu can stay!' said Thug.

Soon all the rats were squeaking as well. Black Spot made himself small.

'As you say, Skip,' he said.

After that, none of the three sisters had any problems with the rats on board the

Hydromyst. Although Pew had tricked them, they forgave him because of *kree* and because he'd defied Black Spot and given them a place on the ship.

Runa was obviously pleased to see 'ratty'. She squealed with delight when Lu ran up to her and sat on her back legs to say hello.

The Captain gave Runa a cabin and told the crew she was no longer a stowaway but a guest of honour instead. She was allowed to go up on deck and walk around and was given better food than dried bread and water to eat and drink.

The crew let Runa borrow whatever books they had on board, including a bible and copies of Dutch poetry. She spent hours puzzling out their meanings. She learned more words every day, including some her Pa would probably be quite cross to hear about, and soon she and the Captain were good friends.

She still enjoyed Lu's visits the most, though.

'You ought to have a medal, little rat,' she would say. Lu would roll over and let the girl tickle her tummy. From time to time they still played the 'bite-bite' game.

The rest of the voyage was smooth sailing and once the ship was re-rigged, fair winds brought them across to Jamaica.

Lu and Runa were watching on deck as the ship reached the New World. It set down anchor in a small harbour close to Golunda. This was a bustling town surrounded by palm trees and silver beaches. All sorts of people walked up and down the streets. Interesting smells wafted on the breeze.

'I wonder if Pa will get the note,' said Runa. She wasn't allowed off the ship because the Captain did not want her running around a rough and ready Jamaican port town on her own.

The sailors moved up and down the gangway unloading the tools, provisions and mail. The sun started to set.

'Oh, ratty,' said Runa. 'I don't think I'm going to see him.'

She stroked Lu to make herself feel better...

Then a man appeared on the dock. He was middle-aged and looked worried and careworn.

He wore European clothes, which made him look uncomfortable and strange compared to everyone else. He gazed anxiously up at the ship.

Runa saw him.

'Pa!' she shouted.

'Runa!' he said.

She ran down the gangway and into his arms.

Lu couldn't wait any longer. She, Rip and Preen followed Runa off the ship to search for Jamaican food. The air smelled of roasting meat, coconut flesh and other promising things.

As they alighted, a dockworker frowned and turned to one of the sailors of the *Hydromyst*.

'I saw rats coming from your ship. You need a ship's cat on board,' he said.

'No,' said the Second Mate, who had sobered up after a few weeks in the brig. 'We will have no cats, ever.'

The End, for now...

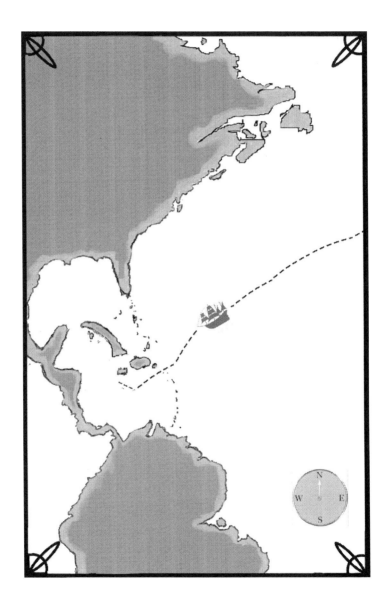

Glossaries

Ship terms:

Aft: The back/behind of the ship

Bilge: The very bottom of the inside of the ship where the filthy water ends up

Bulkhead: A divider or partition between parts of the inside of a ship

Capstan: A wheel used to pull up the anchor or winch ropes tight

Course: A square-ish sail set low on the mast

Fore: The front of the ship

Fluyt: a big cargo ship used very successfully by the Dutch from the 1500s. The *Fluyt* in this story was built in the late 1700s

Hold: Where the cargo, food, tools and other things are kept

Hull: The 'skin' of the ship. Keeps air in and water out (hopefully)

Mainmast: the biggest (normally middle) mast

Orlop: The deck where ropes are stored

Port: On the left, if you are facing forward on a ship

Prow: The very front of the ship, the part that pushes through the sea

Quarterdeck: a small deck. This is the highest deck at the aft of the *Hydromyst*

Scuppers: A gap to allow water to drain from the deck. Rats use them as windows

Starboard: On the right, if you are facing forward on a ship

Tack: A very hard biscuit

Top: A place for sailors or fighters to stand while up a mast. Often mistaken for a crow's nest

Topgallant sail: Above the topsail but not the uppermost sail

Rat terms:

A Mischief: The term for a gang of rats, like a flock of birds or pack of dogs

Bigs: Gigantic two-legged creatures regarded as slow but dangerous. They are messy and leave food around. Otherwise known as 'humans'

Brux/Bruxing: This is when a rat grinds their top and bottom teeth together. It can be a sign of nerves but also of happiness

Buck: A male rat

The Curl: Black Spot's symbol of authority, a piece of gold cloth stolen from a ship officer. Oddly enough, the British Navy later adopted the curl as a sign of high rank. This was a coincidence and had nothing to do with Black Spot

Doe: A female rat

Kree: The rat word for the code they live by to keep peace

Pet: A rat that has given up its wild life to spend time with Bigs. Frowned upon by wild rats

Ritten: A baby rat. Used sometimes instead of the 'true' term *kitten* to avoid them getting mixed up with baby cats

Skip: The leader of the ship rats, the equivalent of a human captain or 'skipper'

Sniff-sniff: A polite greeting. Sniffing allows one rat to find out who the other rat is and what they have been up to

Wild rat: A rat that does not trust or spend time with Bigs

Endnote

Rats have had a very poor reputation over the years. They are still often regarded as dangerous pests, thieves and carriers of disease. Because of this, they are generally the baddies in stories, although there are occasional goodie rats as well. Rats don't sail boats like Ratty from The Wind in the Willows, do karate like Master Splinter from the Teenage Mutant Ninja Turtles or cook gourmet food like Remy from Ratatouille in real life. But did you know there are actual hero rats out there today?

In fact, an organisation called APOPO trains African giant pouched rats (nicknamed HeroRATs!) to detect hidden land mines so they can be safely destroyed, and to sniff out Tuberculosis, a very infectious disease, to help stop its spread. Although they are only very distantly related to brown (Norwegian) rats like Lu, Preen and Rip, African giant pouched rats are just as curious and clever. They are cheap to train, have an excellent sense of smell and are light enough to walk across minefields without setting the explosives off (so they never get hurt).

This book has been released to support the work of APOPO and its HeroRATs. Please consider adopting a HeroRAT, donating to the organisation or letting other people know about this book and the work APOPO rats do. Visit **support.apopo.org** to find out more.

This book was written on a not-for-profit basis. Approximately 50p from each sale will go to APOPO. The rest of the cover price covers the costs of printing and distribution. Amounts may vary according to the publishing format you have chosen to purchase.

You can find out more about the author at www.rhianwriting.wordpress.com, at www.facebook.com/RhiWaller or follow the ratty sisters on Twitter at @LuSniffy. The author has no official links to APOPO. Thank you for reading this story.

About the author:

Rhian Waller was born in Lincolnshire, grew up in North Wales and is a lecturer and occasional freelance journalist in Chester.

She is interested in almost everything and enjoys writing, reading, martial arts, bush craft training, travel, live music, hill walking, SCUBA diving and gaming.

Leeloo, Priss and Ripley, the rats who inspired this book, were adopted from the RSPCA and live in Chester. They like sunflower seeds and snoozing in hammocks.

What did you think of the book? Remember, reviews are like 'tips' for authors. Please consider sharing your thoughts on Amazon.com or Goodreads.com.

Find out what happens next in:

Pirats:
A tale of Mutiny on the High Seas
OUT NOW.